INCOGNITO MOSQUITO

PRIVATE INSECTIVE

"He's fantas-tick!"   —*The New York Slimes*

"This guy doesn't ants around."

—*Playbug*

"You mite give him a buzz."

—*Buzziness Week*

INCOGNITO MOSQUITO

PRIVATE INSECTIVE

by E.A. HASS

ILLUSTRATED BY DON MADDEN

BULLSEYE BOOKS · ALFRED A. KNOPF
New York

Dr. M. Jerry Weiss, Distinguished Service Professor of Communications at Jersey City State College, is the educational consultant for Bullseye Books. A past chair of the International Reading Association President's Advisory Committee on Intellectual Freedom, he travels frequently to give workshops on the use of trade books in schools.

For N. H., who always thought I could,
even when I didn't,
to N., on coming home,
and M., for just being.

The story you are about to read is true. Not even the names have been changed to protect the guilty—or the innocent, for that matter. It is a tale about the FBI, CIA, and BLT. It is the story of notorious insect no-goodniks who are so mean that they make onions cry. It is a book about bug thugs so rotten that they would stab you in the back, and then report you to the police for carrying a concealed weapon.

This is *not* a book about life and death, war and peace, Laurel and Hardy, or peanut butter and jelly. But you can't have everything. The multitalented Incognito Mosquito, Private Insective, certainly doesn't. But, then again, he doesn't miss much!

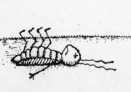

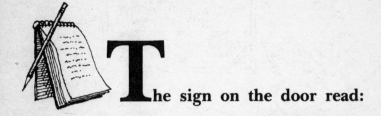

The sign on the door read:

INCOGNITO MOSQUITO
PRIVATE INSECTIVE
"NO CASE TOO SMALL OR HAS TOO MANY LEGS"
THE INSECTIVE IS **IN**

No one answered my knock, so I went on in. As a cub reporter for a well-read underground newspaper, I was supposed to do an article on this Mosquito character. I was last in line when the assignments were handed out.

The Insective was easy enough to find. He was sacked out, feet neatly propped against his desk. "They ought to run this story in the leisure section," I thought to myself. "It's gonna be a real sleeper."

The sleepee awoke with a start. "It" (and I use the term loosely) was wearing a stunning three-quarter-length evening dress. The remaining quarter was 100% hairy legs. "Love your outfit," I said, after introducing myself.

"Oh, thanks," my host(ess) replied. "It's a designer original created especially for me. A bonus from one of the many satisfied customers whose lives I've made a little bit brighter by just being myself, Incognito Mosquito, Private Insective. Yes," he said, fingering the tassels on his gown, "this private insective game certainly has its fringe benefits. Actually, the story that goes with this dress is quite interesting. It should make a good start for your article."

1
The Mysterious Case of the Unsafe Safe

It was the 31st of April, a beautiful spring day. The sun was shining, the birds were singing, the flowers were blooming, and my telephone was ringing. My secretary, Ladybug, had the day off, as usual.

I answered the phone like I always do when she's not here.

I say, "Click, click . . . hummmmmmmmmm. . . . Congratulations, whoever you are. You have reached the Incognito Mosquito Private Insective Agency. No case too small! This is Mr. Mosquito's answering machine talking. Mr. M. is out solving a life-or-death case right now, but if you would like to leave a message, he will get back to you when he gets out of the shower. Don't speak until you hear the buzz. Thank you." Then comes my favorite part. I wait a minute, and then I say, "Buzz." Sometimes, just to throw them off the track, I don't say "buzz" at all. Boy, that really bugs 'em!

Well, anyway, this time I'd just gotten started when a loud, angry voice cut me short, saying, "Mosquito, you were given a nose to breathe through so that you could keep your mouth shut." Right away I recognized my old faithful friend and fellow crime fighter, Inspector Insector. He's one of my biggest fans. I have almost as much respect for him as he has for me.

"What can I do for you, Chief?" I asked sweetly.

There was a moment of silence, and then, in a whisper, he replied, "Don't tempt me, Mosquito! How soon can you be at Bambugger's department store?"

I thought for only an instant. "You need my help on a case, don't you, Chief? Am I hot or cold?"

"As far as I'm concerned, Mosquito, you're about as much help as a glass eye at a keyhole, but my orders were to bring you in on the case. You should have been here two hours ago."

"Well," I said, "that might be tough, but I'll see what I can do. I guess the fastest way to get there would be by helicopter.

You know what they say," I chuckled, "the whirlybug catches the worm!"

I heard a loud click. It took me only a minute to figure out that the conversation had ended. I took off right away for Bambugger's and had no problems except for a quick run-in (run-out, run-in, run-out, run-in) with the revolving doors at the front of the store. I took the elevator right to the Presidential Hive and found the Inspector and Mr. Bambugger himself waiting for me.

"Mr. Mosquito, I'm so glad you were able to squeeze us into your busy schedule. The Inspector here was just telling us about some of your more unusual cases. He assures us that what you are missing in intelligence, you more than make up for in stupidity. I just can't tell you how that makes me feel," Mr. Bambugger said, with a peculiar look on his face.

"Thank you, Mr. B.," I said. "I wish everyone felt the way you and the Inspector do." It did not take long for my superbly trained eye to spot a couple of extra bugs in the room. One was a woman, and the other wasn't. The woman had this incredible set of sparkling white teeth. Dozens of them! I had to shield my eyes from the glare.

The man wasn't much easier to look at. His jeans were so tight, I couldn't tell whether he was on the inside trying to get out, or on the outside trying to get in!

Mr. Bambugger stepped forward. "Mr. Incognito Mosquito, Private Insective, may I introduce the world-famous fashion designers Glorious Vanderbug and Vidal Cocoon."

Ms. Vanderbug smiled. She didn't have any other choice. "How are you, Mr. Mosquito?" she asked politely. Without waiting

for an answer, she went on. "Mr. Cocoon and I are not at all well. The most terrible thing has happened. Early this morning all of the sketches for our new fall lines of clothing were stolen from the safe right here in Mr. Bambugger's office. Do you know what that means? I'll tell you what that means. Tell him what that means, Vidal."

"What that means, Mr. Mosquito, is that

if we don't get those sketches back, half of the best-dressed insect colonies will be running around naked this year!"

I had only a moment to wonder which half he was referring to before Ms. Vanderbug began pleading, "I can't tell you how important those sketches are. They must be found—at any price! Can you help us?"

"I'm sure I can," I said modestly. "Why don't you sit down and give me the facts, ma'am, just the facts."

Ms. Vanderbug began her story tearfully. "Vidal and I had scheduled a meeting with Mr. Bambugger for nine o'clock this morning. Mr. B. arrived early as usual. He found a man knocked out on the floor of his office. This was not usual. Just then, Mr. Cocoon and I came in, and the three of us managed to wake him up. After a few minutes he was able to tell us what happened:

"His name is Herman the Vermin. He

works for Bambugger's as a night cleaning careticker. He had finished his work early this morning and put away his mops and brooms. Then he put on his coat and gloves and got ready to leave. As he stood waiting for the elevator, he heard noises coming from Mr. Bambugger's office.

"Like the good, faithful employee that he is, he went to the end of the hall to check it out. He had just stepped into the room when he was hit from behind and knocked out. We found a dented flyswatter next to him on the floor, but it had been wiped

clean of fingerprints. The door to Mr. Bam-bugger's safe had been blown off, and the sketches were gone!"

"I just don't understand how something like this could have happened," Mr. Bam-bugger sighed. "This building is one hundred percent theftproof, one hundred percent waterproof, and one hundred per-cent fireproof."

"Shame it's not one hundred percent foolproof," Inspector Insector said sharply, throwing a meaningful glance in my direc-tion.

I smiled. "In other words," I said, "this building is one hundred percent proof."

"Naturally," Bambugger replied, "only the best of termites dine here. We're even one hundred percent soundproof. Why, someone could drop a bomb in the next room and you'd never even know it."

Just then, Mr. Bambugger's private secretary came into the room. "Sorry to disturb you, sir," she said, "but I thought you'd like to know that someone just dropped a bomb in the next room."

"What did I tell you?" asked Mr. Bambugger.

"What really bugs me, Mr. Mosquito, is that the thief managed to get out of the store carrying the sketches. You see, everyone—and I do mean everyone—is searched right down to their you-know-whats before leaving the building. You do know what, don't you, Mr. Mosquito?" Cocoon gazed at me expectantly.

I nodded knowingly, afraid to open my mouth for fear that my foot would fall out.

Cocoon continued, "As I was saying, Ms. Vanderbug, Mr. Bambugger himself, and of course yours truly were all searched. There are no exceptions. Never! Never! Never!"

"Tell me," I said, feeling a sudden violent attack of genius coming on, "where is Herman the cleaning vermin now?"

Mr. Bambugger spoke up quickly. "I had him rushed to the hospital in an ambulance. Poor thing, he was really shaken up. Do you have to bother him with questions just now? He's had a hard night, you know."

"Just one question," I said, closing my eyes and crossing my antennae in deep thought as I paced back and forth. The scene was set. I could see it all now. I ran through every step of the crime down to the tiniest detail. I was hot on the track. It was only a matter of time before I brought the guilty party to his—or her—knees! My mind was off and running. There was no way to stop me. Nothing escaped me. I didn't miss a single clue. I never do.

I didn't miss the Inspector's foot, either. Before I knew it, I found myself flat on my back looking up into his eyes. They were not happy eyes.

"Mosquito!" he screamed as his face turned a lovely shade of purplish-green. "Your brain is so small that if I gave you a penny for your thoughts you'd owe me change!"

"Sorry, Chief," I replied. "I'm afraid I don't have change for a penny. In fact, I don't think I have any cents at all. But I do have a question for Herman. I'd like to ask him what he did with the sketches he stole from Mr. Bambugger's safe." I yawned. "Incognito," I said to myself, "you've done it again!"

HOW DID INCOGNITO KNOW
THAT HERMAN THE VERMIN DID IT?

Mr. Bambugger's office was so sound-proof that you couldn't hear a bomb exploding in the next room. Yet Herman said he had heard noises in Mr. Bambugger's office as he stood waiting for the elevator, even though it was down at the end of the hall. Herman wasn't telling the truth.

After stealing the sketches, he hit himself over the head with the flyswatter for three reasons:

1. The only way he could get the sketches out of the building without being searched was to be carried out on a stretcher to an ambulance.

2. He wanted to make doubly sure that no one could possibly suspect him of having stolen the sketches. Thinking that he had been knocked out by the real thief, everyone felt sorry for him.

3. He wanted the day off.

There were no fingerprints on the fly-swatter because Herman was wearing his coat and *gloves*, remember?

The office door swung open, and an attractive young thing stepped in to drop some official-looking documents in Mr. Mosquito's lap. "Please allow me to introduce my charming secretary and admirer from afar, Ladybug," he said sweetly, smiling up at her.

"Mr. Mosquito," she said firmly, frowning down at him, "I've asked you time and time again to stop calling me Ladybug. The name is Ms. Womanbug. Please don't make me remind you again!"

"Ladybug, Ladybug. Why don't you drop this women's lib stuff? There's no way women will ever be equal to men. Admit it. Deep down inside, don't you sometimes wish you were a man?"

"Don't you?" Ms. Womanbug countered neatly.

"This male-female stuff is all very confusing to me," the red-faced Mosquito muttered. "Now, blackmail—that's a different story. Them's my kinda people. Which, as coincidence would have it, brings me to another interesting case."

2
Whatever Happened to Mickey Mantis?

I had just curled up by the fire, good book in hand, ready for a relaxing evening at home, when I was startled by a frantic pounding at my door. It took several minutes to unlock the thirteen ingenious

27

security devices of my own invention without tripping thirteen ingenious burglar alarms, also of my own invention.

When I was finally able to open the door, my exhausted visitor nearly fell on the floor in a faint. I immediately recognized Phineas J. Phleabody, owner of one of the biggest baseball clubs in the league. He handed me this note:

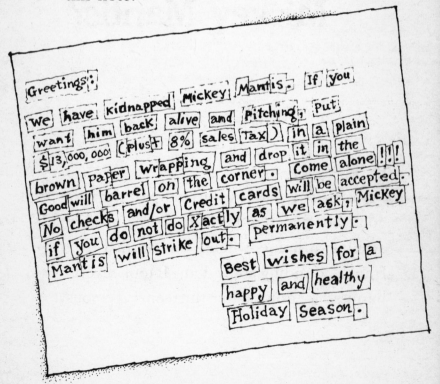

Greetings:

We have kidnapped Mickey Mantis. If you want him back alive and Pitching, Put $13,000,000 (plus 8% sales Tax) in a plain brown paper wrapping and drop it in the Goodwill barrel on the corner. Come alone!!! No checks and/or Credit cards will be accepted. if You do not do Xactly as We ask, Mickey Mantis will strike out. permanently.

Best wishes for a happy and healthy Holiday Season.

The note came in a black envelope. My antennae twitched as I closed my eyes in deep concentration. "Mr. Phleabody," I said softly, "this letter is marked SPECIAL DELIVERY. Am I correct in assuming that the postman just delivered it specially?" Mr. Phleabody nodded. "Hmmmm," I continued, studying the envelope, "black mail, just as I suspected!"

Mr. Phleabody was speechless, obviously awed by my amazing mental capacity and astonishingly quick train of thought. In fact, I've been told on more than one occasion that you can actually see the wheels turning inside my head, and the smoke pouring out of my ears. Finally Mr. Phleabody was able to utter a few words.

"Mosquito," he said, "if I don't play ball with these guys, they'll kill Mantis, and his fans will kill me. I don't know how I'll come up with that kind of money, but if I don't, those guys will fix it so that Mickey won't be able to catch a cold, much less a fly ball!"

"Calm, Phleabody, calm. That's the secret to being a good private insective. You're too nervous. First things first. Here's the game plan. We'll go to the bank and get them to lend you the money. We'll follow the instructions in the ransom note exactly—letter by l-e-t-t-e-r . . . with one minor league exception. I'll be watching every move you make. When our friends get to first base and pick up the load, I'll call 'Foul play' and we'll throw the bums out."

Early the next A.M., Mr. Phleabody set out with the money. I followed closely behind, but somehow I got in front of him and had to tail him walking backward. Even with that complication, everything ran according to schedule. I had decided to wear my helpless, mild-mannered little old lady disguise so that no one would notice me.

And no one did, except for one gentleman, who turned out to be a purse snatcher. I totaled him with a swift sting chop from my "registered as lethal weapon" stinger. It was a reflex action—I just couldn't help myself. I looked around to make sure no one was watching and dragged him off the street and hid him behind some bushes. No one would have paid any attention to a purse snatcher beating up a defenseless little old lady. An elderly woman socking it to a thief might have aroused some suspicion and prompted a call to the local police. I couldn't risk blowing my cover.

Just as I was washing my hands of the unfortunate snatcher, a couple of Bug Scouts came and tried to help me across the street. Bodily. I had a hard time convincing them I didn't want their help.

By the time I caught up with Mr. Phleabody, he had dropped the money in the

Goodwill barrel as directed and was walking away. I sat down on a nearby park bench, ready to assume an ever vigilant and alert, yet shyly old-ladylike pose for however long was necessary.

The sound of screeching tires woke me. I caught a glimpse of three shady-looking characters speeding around the corner in

34

a long, lean, black sedan. Suddenly shots rang out from the car windows, narrowly missing me!

Without wasting a second, I set my mind on instant replay and ran through the episode frame by frame. I always carry a bag of popcorn for just such an occasion. (I hate sitting through a movie without munchies.)

What was bothering me about those sinister faces staring out at me from the black limo?

Suddenly I had it! I yelled, "CUT!" Everyone in the park turned around and pointed at me. Boy, was my face red! But I had it. By running through my mental bug-thug-mug index, I had identified the faces in the car. They belonged to none other than the infamous Criminal Cricket, his dastardly sidekick, Mobster Moth, and their notorious chauffeur, master of the fast getaway, Quick Flee McGee. Together they formed one of the "most wanted" organized crime syndicates of all time—a mob that struck fear into the hearts of honest bugs everywhere—THE UNSQUISHABLES.

I knew what I was up against. I had to get ready. Without wasting another moment, I tore off my not-so-defenseless-little-old-lady disguise and made a beeline for Cricket Castle. A spectacular vine-covered

mansion tucked away in a shady neighborhood several hours out of town, Cricket
Castle had been getting such rave reviews
as *the* exclusive hideaway for fugitives and
their loved ones that you now needed a
reservation.

I was greeted at the door by a stuffed

shirt who went by the curious name of Butler. He ushered me into a magnificent, sunny, high-ceilinged room filled with plants of every size, shape, and color—a regular planetarium.

Suddenly I heard a faint rustling behind me. I spun around at dizzying speed. Could I have walked into a Venus's-flytrap? Was this to be the end of me?? And what about Mickey Mantis, Mom's apple pie, truth, justice, and the American way??? After the room stopped spinning, I found myself face to face with my infamous enemy, the ever popular Criminal Cricket. "So-o-o-o-o, how's the wife, C.C.?" I asked casually, hoping to throw him off guard.

"Come now, Mosquito," Criminal replied. "You and I have known each other too long for that. Don't expect me to believe this is just a friendly social call. What's on your, if you'll forgive the expression, mind?"

"Just this, C.C., ole pal. A couple of hours ago I was used as target practice by some guys who used to be in your employ. I've been working on the Mickey Mantis kidnapping. Perhaps you've read about it in the papers? Funny thing, too—one of the bullets I recovered happened to be just your caliber!"

"My ex-caliber, you mean," C.C. said innocently. "Why, I haven't used a heater—I mean, a lethal firearm-type weapon—since I won a Kewpie doll for my niece at a local shooting gallery."

"Yes, I remember it well. You shot the owner of the gallery and stole the doll." I smiled pleasantly.

"Those days are behind me, Mosquito. Now I'm a respectable businessman, owner of Gyp-sy Moth Limited, Inc. It's the first chain of drive-in fortunetellers to go nationwide," C.C. boasted proudly. "I supply the glass doorknobs—I mean, crystal balls—and the member moths provide the pigeons—er, ah, customers."

Even though I didn't believe a word C.C. was feeding me, I decided to go along for the ride. My superior powers of defective reasoning told me that this drive-in fortunetelling biz was just a dishonest front to cover up C.C.'s other illegal doings. "Gee, that's quite a racket, Ricket . . . uhm, er, ah . . . cracket, Cricket . . . hmmm, ugh . . . cricket, Cracket. Anyway, that's quite a good deal you've got there. Funny thing, though, you know. I could swear that the other gentleman who shot at me was none other than your old pal and partner in slime, Mobster Moth. Say, whatever happened to the ole gang, anyhow? The Unsquishables were a great bunch of thugs."

C.C. smiled faintly. A misty look came over his eyes. "I'm afraid I haven't kept the touch on them—oh, excuse me—I mean, in touch with them. You know, I've turned over a new leaf, and they're still crawling around in the dirt, so to speak. What a waste of hidden talent! Besides, I've been out of town for several months on a fortunetelling junket. In fact, I got back home from the airport only a minute before you dropped in for our little chat. Oh, goodness me! Where are my manners today?"

"Maybe you left them on the plane," I suggested helpfully.

My host graciously continued, wisely choosing to ignore me. "Here we've been babbling away about old times, and I haven't offered you any refreshments. I'm afraid there isn't much around. I haven't had a chance to restock yet, but whatever I've got is yours for the asking. Tell me, what can I get you?"

"That's a dangerous question, C.C.," I

said, playing for time. "Just some coffee would be fine."

"Right. I'll be back in a minute. Please make yourself at home." C.C. turned and hurried out into the kitchen. If I'd been at home I would have taken off my shoes, put my feet up, and turned on the TV. Since C.C. didn't have a TV, I decided to take advantage of his absence and quickly scanned the room for any hidden clues to the whereabouts of the missing Mantis. So far I was batting zero, but I hadn't struck out yet.

The two suitcases standing in the corner of the room seemed to verify C.C.'s story of just having returned from a trip. However, one of the first lessons we learned in

private insective school was that things aren't always what they seem. I didn't want to jump to any confusions before checking out all of the possible evidence. Then I could make a fool out of myself with a clear conscience, knowing that I had done my best.

Before I could continue the search my host returned, carrying a stunning antique silver coffee service. Carefully placing it on the table, he sat, leaned forward in his chair, and inquired politely, "Milk or sugar? Hemlock? A dash of cyanide perhaps?"

"Just a bit of milk, please," I said, glancing around the room uneasily. I was groping for a clue—any clue—that would put me back in the ole ball game. Preoccupied, I took a sip of coffee. I was beginning to get worried. It had never taken me this long to solve a case of blackmail. All I asked for was a stroke or two of 100% pure, organic, undiluted genius. Was that too much to ask?

Could I be slipping? Losing my touch? What a horrible way to go.

I was just on the verge of handing in my badge, bat, ball, and glove when suddenly it came to me. A grin slowly spread across my devilishly handsome face. Cunningly, as always, I excused myself, asking for the "little mosquitoes' room." Out of C.C.'s earshot, I called the Inspector to tell him that another case was packed and ready for takeout. Yes, it was time to send another poor unfortunate fugitive from justice to the slammer for extra innings—lots of extra innings!

Returning to my seat, I looked Criminal Cricket right in the eye and spoke these exact words: "You set a fine table, C.C. Unfortunately you also lie, cheat, steal, and bite your fingernails." C.C. stared at his hands in shame. "I hereby accuse you of kidnapping Mickey Mantis and of taking potshots at a defenseless little old lady, who just happened to have the misfortune of being me at the time. You pitched a perfect game—except for one error. And that error is going to cost you the game."

Another archenemy of the insect world had just struck out.

WHAT WAS C.C.'S ONE MISTAKE?

Criminal Cricket struck out by being *too* hospitable. He told Incognito that he had just returned from a several-months'-long trip and hadn't even gotten a chance to go to the market. Yet he offered Incognito coffee—*with milk in it!* If that milk had been sitting in C.C.'s fridge for more than a week or two at most, it would have been too sour for even Incognito to drink.

After deducing that Criminal Cricket had not been out of town at all, our hero realized that the suitcases he had spotted earlier were actually packed and ready for a quick getaway. Having collected the ransom for Mickey Mantis, C.C. was preparing to fly the coop.

Mickey Mantis was returned to his waiting fans at the stadium.

Criminal Cricket was returned to his waiting cell in solitary.

"That was the wildest story yet, Mr. Mosquito," I said, properly impressed.

"Oh, that's nothing," my host assured me. "I get better as I go along. I've got a reputation for digging up cases in the weirdest places. Hmmm . . . let me see if I can recall some of my, shall we say, more 'unusual' cases. . . ."

3
The Case of the Vanishing Magician

Ah, yes! Have I ever told you about the time I was called over to Sting Sting Prison? Seems they needed some outside help on an inside job. Or was it some inside help on an outside job? Oh, well, no matter. Whichever it was, I gave it to them—but good! It happened like this:

Every year all of the wardens from the different prisons get together for a big conference—a regular detention convention. Well, this particular year it was being hosted by Sting Sting, an institution famous for its anti-escape campaign and strict no-gambling policy. Ten to one you'd never get out of there alive.

The only escape attempt made within the last ten years was when a chain gang tried to sneak past the guards by posing as a giant charm bracelet. And they almost made it, too. It wasn't until they were on their way out the front gates that they were fingered by the long arm of the law.

Anyway, the Warden, one I. Witless, decided to involve the prisoners in the festivities this year—to turn it into your basic incarceration celebration. He expected to show off how successfully his rehabilitation program helped hardened criminals become useful members of society. He did not expect one of these hardened criminals to rehabilitate himself right out of the prison gates!

The Warden had planned a talent show featuring the prisoners. The Flying Fleanis did their famous acrobatic act. It was an encore of the performance that got them

THE
FLYING
FLEANIS

ninety-nine years with an option for ninety-nine more for The Great Snobbery Robbery. You remember, don't you? It was that charity ball to raise money for needy fruit flies with a vitamin C deficiency. Everyone who was anyone was there, and anyone who was there was robbed.

Warden Witless had combed the prison looking for talent. The lineup was really outstanding. There was even a skit from that terrific late-night TV show *Saturday Night Hive,* with Steve "I'm a wild and crazy fly" Martin.

The last act on the program was a magic routine to be performed by a trickster who billed himself as Houdunit. He turned out to be none other than the notorious Felonious Fly, terror of the free skies, wanted for mass insecticide. The magic was anything but routine. Talk about your sleight of hand! This character was so shifty, every

time he shook your hand you had to count
your fingers.

His big finale was really quite spectacular. While the entire audience watched, he
had the prisoners wheel a large platform
on stage. He invited the wardens to inspect
it carefully to make sure it was 100% solid,
with no trap doors or other mechanical escape devices. Then he sat on the platform.

Next he had men lug in huge stones and directed them to construct a small room, walling him in on all four sides. A sheet of steel covered the top of the tiny room, and it, too, was covered with the heavy rocks.

Any attempt to remove even one of the huge stones would surely have caused the entire structure to tumble down, leading to a very squishy death for its lone occupant.

From inside, Houdunit dramatically announced his intentions. Mystery and suspense mounted in his voice with every word. He planned to dematerialize, pass through the solid wall, and rematerialize on the outside of the stone cube. "So what?" you might say. A magician's trick? Maybe. But the interesting part is that Houdunit disappeared . . . and never reappeared!

After several minutes of patient waiting, the audience began to get antsy. Nothing seemed to be happening with the cube—

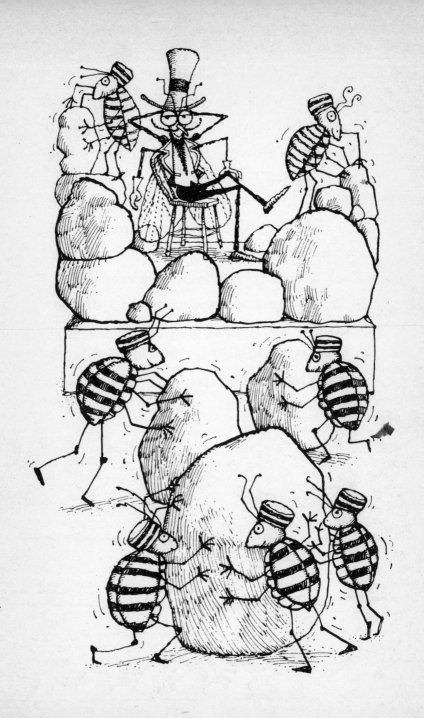

either inside or out. There's nothing worse than a horde of bored wardens. Finally Warden Witless ordered the stone room taken apart for an official rock-to-rock search. He wanted no stone left unturned. It was slow work removing the heavy stones one by one and rolling them off the stage. Rock & roll, rock & roll, rock & roll.

When the last rock was rolled, the audience was left staring at an empty stage. They rubbed their eyes in disbelief. Nothing was left on the bare platform. Houdunit *had* done it! He had done the impossible!

He had vanished into thin air and escaped from Sting Sting, leaving not a clue to be found.

The wardens in the audience laughed. The prisoners cheered. Warden I. Witless cried like a baby. Fortunately, before he broke down completely, he had the presence of mind to do what I would have done if faced with a similar situation. He called me.

I arrived on the spot almost immediately. My old archadmirer, Inspector Insector, was waiting for me. I smiled warmly. He frowned

VISITING WARDENS   I. WITLESS WARDEN   INSPECTOR

coldly. In as few words as possible, he spit out the story, choking on every syl-la-ble.

I waited politely until he had finished. "Forgive me," I said humbly, throwing in a dash of embarrassment just for good measure. "I'm afraid I'm a bit absentminded—"

"You said it, not me," the Inspector interrupted with an evil grin, happy for a change.

"Right," I continued. "As I was saying . . . could you refresh my memory on one minor point? The rocks that were used to wall in Houdunit—where are they now?"

I could tell the Inspector was thrown by the question. He shook his head sadly. "Mosquito, it's at times like this that I wish your parents had never met."

"Funny, you're not the first person who's said that, Chief," I said. "But now, on to a lighter subject. What about the rocks?"

"For your information, Mr. Mosquito,"

the Inspector explained in a tense voice, "said rocks are back at the prison mine. Tomorrow they're due to be shipped from the rock pile to the site of a new shopping mall. But I don't see what difference it makes." Wearily he added, "You're about as much help as an eye doctor at a potato farm!"

"Interesting point, Chief," I said cheerfully. "My mother always wanted me to be an optimist. In fact, things are looking up already. I'm pretty sure you will find your quarry in the quarry!"

HOW DID INCOGNITO KNOW WHERE TO FIND HOUDUNIT?

Incognito realized that one of the stones used to wall in Houdunit must have been hollow! Since the rocks were mined by the inmates at the prison quarry, this could easily have been arranged.

On the surface the special stone looked just like all the rest. It was built into the wall right under the noses of the visiting wardens. Hidden from the audience's view, Houdunit opened up the hollowed-out rock and climbed inside. He had been planning this caper for a long time. The rock was custom-made. It had all the comforts of home. More, even.

Houdunit knew that the stones would be returned to the prison quarry and soon afterward be sent to the site of the new shopping mall. Houdunit figured that all he had to do was sit tight until the stores opened!

Unfortunately for him, Incognito saw to it that the only accommodations his performance rated was his old room at the Sting Sting Sheraton.

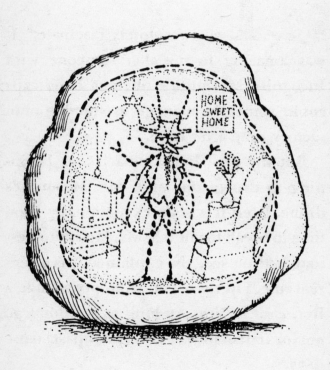

I was absolutely fascinated. It was amazing to me that someone with Incognito Mosquito's obvious handicaps could somehow manage to stumble onto victory time after time.

But my growling stomach was beginning to drown out even Mr. Mosquito's drone. I felt it was an exceptionally good time to break for lunch. Mr. Mosquito hesitated. "You see," he explained, "as a general rule, I never eat on an empty stomach. But, *c'est la flea.* As long as we don't go out for Italian food. I'm very antipasta these days."

We locked the office door behind us and started down the stairs. Before I knew it, Mr. Mosquito was tumbling helplessly down the two flights to the street below. He landed, slightly more dazed than usual, in an upright position. "What's all the racket about?" he asked in a confused tone. "I thought this was supposed to be a quiet neighborhood. How's a person to get any work done around here?"

I scraped the crumbled bug off the sidewalk and steered him toward the restaurant of his choice. Once seated, he turned to me and whispered, "You'll love this place. All us private insective types eat here. Everyone is so busy trying not to be noticed, it's hard to tell the customers from the wallpaper."

Mr. M. ordered the Incognito Mosquito Special. "It's a triple-decker sandwich named for me—half turkey, half ham," he

explained proudly. I ordered a steak sand-wich on whole wheat with a side of horse-radish. I hoped it would get the bad taste out of my mouth. Little did I know that the bad taste was not in my mouth, but sitting across the table.

As soon as the waitress had gone, Mr. Mosquito smiled dreamily and said, "Whenever anyone even mentions the word HORSEradish, I can't help but think of one of my finest hours."

"And which finest hour was that?" I questioned bitterly. "I'm sure you have whole days of them."

"True, true," Mr. Mosquito responded modestly. "But this time I was thinking of the McMillipede case. You see, I had a real 'steak' in it."

Maximillion
McMillipede

4
The Bizarre Barbecue Affair

It was one of my most challenging cases. Even for me. I had received an urgent telegram from Maximillion McMillipede, millionaire heir. You may recall, he's that fabulously wealthy Texan who doubled his fortune in Ant Hill-tons and Roach Palaces. It seems there was a highly organized horsefly-rustling ring operating in his backyard. He forgot to mention, of course, that his backyard was half of the Midwest!

McMillipede wanted me to fly down immediately. I've got to admit, I was a bit nervous about taking the job because of my allergy to horses. I'd suffered from broncitis ever since I was a kid. But at the last minute I decided to try and ride it out. I wired McMillipede that I could make no guarantees, but would put some feelers out and see what I could rustle up.

As I taxied down the landing runway at the private airport, a terrific clatter assaulted my eardrums. Maximillion McMillipede had come out to meet me personally. Have you ever heard the racket one thousand spurs make? McMillipede was

your basic economy-size Texan. He grabbed
my wrist and shook me vigorously for several minutes. Then he delivered a slap on
my back that nearly knocked my socks off.
His mother had obviously taught him to
shake well before bruising.

"Ma friends call me Big Mac," he boomed.

"My friends call me Incognito. And I wish I were."

Ushering me into the sprawling McMillipede mansion, Big Mac continued, "This here is ma darlin' daughter, Mary Margaret McMillipede—M.M.M.M. for short. I sent for you, Mr. Mosquitter, because her prize

horsefly has been stole and it's darn near broke her little heart."

"Yes, I see, Mr. McMillipede . . . er, augh, gee whiz, I mean . . . Big Mac. Tell me, just when did this happen?"

"Why, she's been ma daughter ever since she was born!" Big Mac answered in a surprised voice.

"No, no. I mean, when was the horsefly stolen? Why don't you just relax and start from the beginning." I gritted my teeth patiently for several minutes before I realized mosquitoes don't have teeth.

Big Mac let out his belt a notch, took a deep breath, and told me his story. "Well, this is the way it happened," he began slowly. "I gave ma little chicklet, M.M.M.M. here, one of ma prize thoroughbred horsefly fillies to raise for her Camp Fire Fly project. Fleabiscuit was her name. The horsefly, I mean—not ma daughter.

"Last week this darn horsefly just upped and downright disappeared. And she's not the only one, neither, Mr. Mosquitter. In the last few months or so, over two dozen head of ma best stock have vanished without a trace. They didn't even leave a forwarding address." Big Mac shook his head sadly, brushing away a tear.

"Isn't it the usual practice to brand your herd?" I asked the big fella.

He responded without hesitation. "Does the big wheel roll? Why, if I was to spot any of ma missin' stock, I could identify them in a flash by the 'MM' brand. Lookie here!" he exclaimed, pulling off his left boot to reveal the trademark.
"I keep it handy
so's I won't fergit it.
Once or twice I spotted
a stray horsefly that
I would have

sworn was mine, but it wore a different brand. One of ma cowbugs, Charles Wagon, can tell you more about that than I can."

Big Mac beckoned to a wrangly wrangler standing by the ole corral. "Mr. Incogniter Mosquitter, may I introduce one of my most trusted hands, Chuck Wagon. Tell him what you know, Chuck."

"Well, Mr. Mosquitter, it's not much," Chuck began shyly. "I know every one of these horseflies like the back of my hoof. I could pick out any one of 'em with my antennae tied behind my back. Last week I saw Dirty Hairy in the far pasture with what I know was one of our prize fillies! It made me so mad!"

"I'll take over now. Thanks, Chuck," Big Mac said, steering me into a private corner of the room. "Dirty Hairy is well knowed in these parts. He's an ornery varmint who owns the Barbecue Ranch."

His voice dropped to a whisper. "When I spotted that familiar-lookin' horsefly wearin' a different brand, guess whose brand she was a-wearin'? Yep, you got it. It was Dirty Hairy's brand. The brand of the Barbecue Ranch! I ain't no fancy-pants private insective, but if I was you, I'd start with Dirty Hairy. There ain't none dirtier. But . . . I gotta tell ya, Mr. Mosquitter, this Dirty Hairy's a dangerous outlaw. I didn't want to say anything in front of M.M.M.M., but he has this really nasty habit. You see" —Big Mac gulped uncomfortably—"he has this tendency to, uhmm, er, ah . . . well, eat anything that stands in his way. Don't make any difference what it is, neither— animal, vegetable, mineral, you, me, his mother—he don't care."

"Now, don't worry about me, Mr. Mc-Millipede," I said confidently. "I've come up against this kind of thing before. It's a well-known psychological phenomenon. Obviously a classic case of the Edible Complex."

Big Mac grinned, clearly relieved. "I'm really glad to hear you say that, Mr. Mosquitter. I don't mind tellin' you, when these thefts first started I called in the local law— our sheriff, Wyatt Twerp. He staked out the area, tryin' to round up some of the missin' horsefly flesh, but he couldn't pin a thing on that Dirty Hairy critter. You're ma last hope, Mr. Mosquitter. Sure hope you're not a bum steer!"

I decided to take Big Mac's advice. Shortly before sunup the next morning, I set out in search of Dirty Hairy's hideout on a borrowed burro. Realizing that the only way to check out his operation was to go undercover and become a member of the gang, I wore my Ruthless Cutthroat Rustler/Hustler Outfit #7937a. It's one of my favorites.

It took several days of hard riding (have you ever sat on a burro that long?) before I caught up with the gang. Correction. Before they caught up with me. I was lassoed right off my burro, bound, gagged, hogtied, and horsewhipped before finally being dragged in to see the head honcho.

Greasy spoon city! There were half a dozen moldy characters slinking around the room, each one slimier than the last. In the center was their leader—the bottom of the barrel, the end of the road, the cream of the cheese—Dirty Hairy. Talk about your basic dispose-all! And he smelled like it, too. Mac McMillipede didn't steer me wrong. Dirty Hairy was covered with good ole American filth—surrounded by tremendous piles of rotten veggies, rusty cans, and no-deposit, no-return bottles. I could barely pick him out of the crowd.

"Macho Gazpacho, mon signor," I said

cheerfully. "Allow me to introduce myself. El Mosquito Bandito, at your service. Wanted in fifty-three states, eleven foreign countries, and . . . Hawaii," I announced with great pride. "I am extremely interested in applying for membership in your world-renowned criminal organization. Could you be so kind as to inform me as to any vacancies which might be available at the present time?"

"Huh?" my cultured host replied.

"I have references from the most unreliable of sources."

That must have done the trick. De-slouching himself, Dirty Hairy cleared his throat with all the alleged dignity he could muster. He began graciously, "As coincidence would have it, sir, one of our former members has recently 'checked out,' so to speak. After carefully reviewing your credentials, I take great pride in offering you this position with open arms and closed wallet."

"Thank you, sir. I am truly honored. I will do my best to make you proud of me, and follow the code of trickery, dishonesty, and deceit to the best of my ability." Secretly, of course, I congratulated myself for infiltrating the gang. But before I had the chance to shake my hand, Dirty Hairy suggested that we all go out and have a drink to celebrate.

My new employer ordered: "Tick-quila Stingers all around."

"And one milk, please."

Suddenly there was a deadly silence. All eyes in the room were focused on me. Immediately I realized I'd goofed. I knew I'd have to recover quickly or I would blow my cover—and Dirty Hairy would blow my head off.

"Make it a double," I growled. "And put

it in a dirty glass." Instantly the room came alive with the sound of slurping. I had said the right thing and everything was OK once more. Whew! That was a close one!

"Coffee break is over, gentlemen," Dirty Hairy said suddenly a few minutes later. "This place looks like siesta city. Wake up! Time to make some dishonest money! El Mosquito Bandito, you come with me to the corral."

"OK, corral. Right, D.H.," I said brightly,
waving gaily to the gang. "Hasta lumbago,
fellas!" I followed Dirty Hairy to a broken-
down corral. The pen held a dozen horseflies, obviously of thoroughbred quality.
"Hot stuff in more ways than one," I said
under my breath.

I was not at all surprised to see that
several of the animals wore Big Mac's
brand. But I still couldn't see

how Dirty Hairy could pull off stealing these horseflies and claiming them as his own, when each animal wore the permanent brand of its real owner.

I didn't have long to wonder, though. Dirty Hairy pointed to the campfire, where several branding irons were heating up, ready for action. He explained the branding procedure to me, step by step. I played dumb. Fortunately it wasn't hard. I'm a rotten actor.

When we were ready to start, two of the slimy seven roped one of the horseflies and maneuvered it into position. Hairy reached for one of the hot branding irons and made a test brand on the nearest unfortunate log. This is how it looked:

All of a sudden I heard a click. If I'd known someone was going to take pictures, I would have combed my hair. Then I realized that the click was coming from inside my head. I said to myself, "Self," I said, "there has got to be a reason for that click. Any bright ideas, genius?" But no answer came. All I got was an echo, bouncing off empty space.

Then suddenly it hit me: the evidence I needed to lock up Dirty Hairy and his gang for life. "Gee, what a shame," I sighed quietly. "I was just getting to like this job!"

WHAT NEW EVIDENCE DID
INCOGNITO UNCOVER TO CONVICT
DIRTY HAIRY AND HIS SLIMY MOB
OF FIRST-DEGREE HORSEFLY RUSTLING?

Incognito saw that the

brand

fit *over* the

brand!

The familiar-looking horseflies that Big Mac had seen on the range actually *were* his animals. Dirty Hairy had just rebranded them and claimed them for his own.

Dirty Hairy and his greasy mob got fifty years, and a lifetime supply of Head & Shoulders.

"To tell you the truth," I.M. said with a straight face, "this private insective game isn't all it's cracked up to be. It's not all money, excitement, glamor, intrigue, wine, women, and song. Almost, but not quite. And then there's danger. We have to learn to live with it, you know. Always fearing for our lives, wondering if today is the tomorrow we'll never see."

I nodded sympathetically, wishing that yesterday was the today I'd never ... Horrified, I stopped myself mid-thought. I was beginning to sound like him!

Meanwhile, Incognito continued, blissfully unaware. "Even our daydreams are nightmares," he said. "Which reminds me. I've got a case you won't want to miss!"

z z z z z z z z z z z z z z z z z z z z Z z z z z Z Z Z Z Z z z z Z

5
The Waterbug Scandal

I was suddenly awakened from a deep sleep by a sharp ping in the stinger. "What the *!&?'#!" I said, mid-snore. Immediately my computerlike brain was off and running. I may be missing a few transistors here and there, but the answer came to me like a flash in the dark. Someone must be recruiting guest celebrities for that new captive audience participation show, *Let's Make a Meal.*

I didn't have much time to think about it though. My ears were ringing and I soon blacked out. At least, I *think* I blacked out. You see, it was already dark in the room, it being night and all, and I had been sleeping and . . . Anyway, it all happened very quickly. The last thing I remember was turning on my answering machine. I didn't want to miss any hot cases while I was out being kidnapped.

When I finally came to, I found myself strapped to an uncomfortable wooden chair. A harsh light glared mercilessly down on me. I heard myself cry out in a hoarse, parched voice, "Sunglasses. Please, I beg of you, sunglasses. Have you no conscience?

I'm not picky. They don't even have to be Polaroid." But it did no good.

The three bug thugs staring down at me were obviously bad news. Their beady eyes, sinister smiles, and receding antennae were all part of the typical criminal profile I had grown to know and love in my years as ace crime fighter. These guys looked so crooked, I figured they screwed their socks on every morning.

Questions filled my mind. Even though there's a lot of vacant space up there, it felt crowded. Soon there was standing room only. Fortunately for everyone present, including myself, I had just been gagged.

Then the torture started. It began when they took off the gag. It was horrible. Too horrible for words. (Besides, this story is rated PG. Maybe next time.) All I can say is that it was even worse than going to the dentist! Twice!

Just as I was about to pass out, a secret panel at the back of the room swung open. There was total silence. A single figure stood outlined against the darkness. After what I'd gone through I wouldn't have recognized my own mother (forgive me, Mom), but I knew, at that moment, that I was looking at a myth.

It spoke. "Mosquito, your intelligence must be the best-kept secret in the entire

department. I myself used the latest brain-washing techniques on you, and all I got were suds. Bubbles. Just empty bubbles."

I smiled. It hurt. I smiled again. In private insective school we took classes in how to smile at pain and laugh at danger. Or was it laugh at pain, smile at danger? Just to be on the safe side I chuckled cautiously. "It's true, Your Mythicness, whenever I go to mind readers, they only charge me half price. With a discount for the young at heart, feeble of brain."

I said to myself, "If this guy went to all that trouble just to try and brainwash me, then there really must be something worth-while up there after all. But . . . could the Inspector have been wrong all these years?"

Meanwhile, the figure silhouetted before me muttered to himself, "Three full pages of private insectives listed in the Yellow Pages and I have to choose one with a storefront brain! Nothing to lose by giving him a test drive, I guess. He can't be any worse than the impression he's already made."

"Incognito Mosquito here," I said.

"The name is F. Flea Bailey, staunch protector of the underbug, defender of the rich and upper middle classes," the silhouette thundered.

"I see you've already met my esteemed colleagues." He nodded toward the sinister-looking lineup. "This is B. Ed Bug, an undercover agent, Lieuten Ant, on special assignment from the Federal Bureau

of Insectigation, and his aide, Corporal Punishment."

"With good guys like these," I thought to myself, "who needs bad guys?"

Bailey continued, "Let me get right to the point, Mosquito. We've had a serious leak in our security over here. We tried to fix it ourselves—called every plumber in the phone book—but it didn't do any good. There was nothing left to do but use Drāno. That's when I thought of you."

"Smart move, F. Flea, baby," I said, smiling modestly. "Best thing you could have done." I didn't know what he was after, but I had nothing to win by not playing along.

A strange look came over F. Flea's face. I've noticed lately that a lot of people get that look when I'm around.

F. Flea sighed wearily. "As I was saying . . . very early this morning a top-security apartment at the Waterbug Arms was bro-

ken into. A briefcase containing several secret fly-papers was stolen. We must get those
documents back at any cost, Mosquito. The
fate of the nation, and possibly the entire
world, including New Jersey, is resting on
your antennae. Don't let us down."

"Tell me, F. Flea, whose apartment was
it? That was burgled, I mean." I wanted to
have all the information at my fingertips so
that when the time came I could just scratch
my head and get the answer. The only
problem with that system is that my mind
is so razor sharp, I have to be careful not
to slit my wrist.

"I was just getting to that, Mosquito. A
little patience, please," Bailey said sharply.
"The apartment belongs to M.Y.O. Beeswax, Secretary of the Inferior."

I was puzzled. "I didn't know Beeswax
was elected Secretary of the Inferior."

"It was a secret ballot," F. Flea explained.

"He was always looking down on everyone, anyway. They just decided to make it official."

He continued, "Unfortunately the honorable Mr. Beeswax was able to catch only a quick glimpse of the intruder escaping through the parking lot in the dawn's early light. Oh, say, you can see I'm afraid his description isn't very detailed, but at least it gives us something to go on. Mr. Beeswax said the burglar was on the small side, wore a dark three-piece suit, and ran with a slight limp.

"Sounds kind of familiar, doesn't it? A little too familiar, if you ask me. It's my hunch that Racketeer Roach is up to his old tricks again. He's tried this kind of thing before, you know."

I didn't say a word. "I'm glad you agree with me, Mosquito," F. Flea said. "I'm going to tell Beeswax that we've got our man. He was very apologetic about not being able to give us more to work with. I assured him that he did much better than most, but he was still pretty uptight about the whole thing. I guess Beeswax feels responsible, you know."

"Can't say that I blame him for feeling responsible," I said. "He is, you know." The slightest hint of a smile danced across my face and disappeared behind my head.

HOW DID INCOGNITO KNOW
THAT BEESWAX WAS THE REAL THIEF?

Remember F. Flea Bailey quoting Mr. Beeswax's description of the burglar as he escaped through the parking lot? The Secretary of the Inferior testified that the thief was wearing a three-piece suit. That means a jacket, pants, and . . . *a vest!* How could Beeswax have known that the burglar had a vest on under his jacket if he only caught a back view of the fleeing intruder?

In his eagerness to play the helpful fly witness, Mr. Beeswax gave himself away! He threw in the part about the limp just for good measure, thinking that it would finger the innocent (for the first time in his life) Racketeer Roach and throw the Insective off the track.

In addition to serving time on robbery charges, the former Secretary of the Inferior is now being sued by Racketeer Roach for defamation of character.

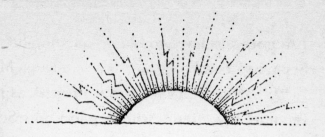

Glancing up from my notes, I saw that the morning sun was already on the rise. I knew I would have to scramble to make my deadline. "Thanks so much for your time, Mr. Mosquito," I said appreciatively, preparing for a hasty retreat. "I'm sure I have enough information in my little black book here to write a humdinger of an article."

Mr. Mosquito smiled warmly. "That's good news. I'm so glad you got what you came for. Now for the bad news. As Shakespeare said, 'You can't take it with you.'*

*"Gee, I don't remember saying that."—Wm. Shakespeare

I'm going to have to burn your notebook. Security, you know.

"What would happen to my practice, my income, my clients who depend on me to defend them when the chips are down, the very essence of my incognitohood? I'd lose the ability to surprise and stun the criminal element. My brilliant career as a private insective would come to an untimely end. Squished in my prime!"

I stared at him in amazement. "I don't understand," I cried as I delivered my precious notes into his waiting hands. Silently I turned and shuffled out of the room, my head hanging in disappointment.

It was not until I was halfway down the block that I reached into my pocket and pulled out my portable tape recorder. I smiled to myself. I had outsmarted the great Incognito Mosquito, Private Insective. I had beaten him at his own game. He never knew he was being bugged.

Back home, seated at my trusty type-writer, I prepared to write the greatest story of my career. I cracked my knuckles for good luck and switched on my trusty tape recorder, grinning with anticipation.

What a shock! I was greeted by the melodic strains of "It's a Small, Small, Very Small, Even Smaller World." Over and over again. Smaller and smaller. Incognito had outsmarted me outsmarting him. No matter how hard I tried, I couldn't blank out the sound of Incognito Mosquito's droning voice rhythmically reminding me, "A fly in the ointment is worth two in the bush."

Fortunately for me, I have what Mr. Mosquito would have called a "photogenic" memory. Fortunately for you, my memory was only photogenic enough to remember the five stories I have so painstakingly (and painfully!) just told you.

As a little token of my appreciation for his unique style of noncooperation, I've handstitched a sampler for Mr. Mosquito to hang on his wall. I will never forget him. As hard as I try. I want him to have something to remember me by too. Always.

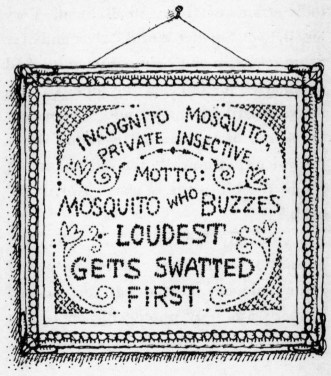

INCOGNITO MOSQUITO, PRIVATE INSECTIVE

MOTTO:

MOSQUITO WHO BUZZES LOUDEST GETS SWATTED FIRST

About the Author

E. A. Hass shares a New York City apartment with two lazy, literate cats. In the summer there are usually several dozen mosquitoes around as well, any one of which could be *the* mosquito.

The idea for Incognito Mosquito, Private Insective, came out of the author's occasional trips to deliver important papers to a downtown office the day before a meeting. This mission would be secretly accomplished in classic messenger disguise—jeans, sweatshirt, and sneakers—your basic "incognito mosquito" outfit. The following day the author would appear all dressed up, ready for the meeting. The boss's secretary would do a double take and ask in a confused voice, "Haven't I seen you somewhere before?" E. A. would simply smile.

About the Artist

Don Madden lives with his wife, son, and daughter in an old farmhouse in upstate New York. They share the place with a large scraggly dog and a small flabby cat, who spend their time trading fleas. Before moving to the country Mr. Madden studied and taught at the Philadelphia Museum College of Art. Now he illustrates children's books and fights off hordes of six-legged visitors.